Published by Ladybird Books Ltd 2010
A Penguin Company
Penguin Books Ltd, 80 Strand, London, WC2R 0RL, UK
Penguin Books Australia Ltd, Camberwell, Victoria, Australia
Penguin Group (NZ), 67 Apollo Drive, Rosedale, North Shore
0632, New Zealand (a division of Pearson New Zealand Ltd)

This book is based on the TV Series 'Peppa Pig'
'Peppa Pig' is created by Neville Astley and Mark Baker
Peppa Pig © Astley Baker Davies/E1 Entertainment 2003
www.peppapig.com

www.ladybird.com

2 4 6 8 10 9 7 5 3 1
Printed in China

Nursery Rhymes and Songs
Picture Book and CD

Every time you hear the bell, turn the page.

Bing Bong Song

We're playing a tune and we're singing a song,
With a bing and a bong and a bing!

Bong, bing, boo, bing, bong, bing,
Bing, bong, bingerly, bongerly boo!

Bong, bing, boo, bing, bong, bing,
Bing, bong, bingerly, bongerly boo!

Bong, bing, boo, bing, bong, bing,
Bing, bong, bingerly, bongerly boo!

Hey Diddle Diddle

Hey diddle diddle,
The cat and the fiddle,
The cow jumped over the moon;
The little dog laughed
To see such fun,
And the dish ran away
With the spoon.

Grandpa's Little Train

Grandpa's little train goes,
Choo, choo, choo!
Choo, choo, choo!
Choo, choo, choo!
Grandpa's little train goes,
Choo, choo, choo!
All day long.

And the piggies on the train go,
Oink, oink, oink!
Oink, oink, oink!
Oink, oink, oink!
And the piggies on the train go,
Oink, oink, oink!
All day long.

It's Raining! It's Pouring!

It's raining, it's pouring,
The old man is snoring.
He bumped his head,
And went to bed,
And he couldn't get up
In the morning.

Incy Wincy Spider

Incy Wincy spider
climbed up the water spout.
Down came the rain
and washed poor Incy out!
Out came the sun
and dried up all the rain.
Now Incy Wincy spider climbed
up the spout again!

Big Balloon

♫ Big balloon, big balloon, ♫
Bigger than the sun and moon.
Flying high in the sky,
Fly and fly and fly and fly!

Mary Had a Little Lamb

Mary had a little lamb,
Its fleece was white as snow;
And everywhere that Mary went,
The lamb was sure to go.

Pat-a-cake! Pat-a-cake!

Pat-a-cake, pat-a-cake,
baker's man.
Bake me a cake
as fast as you can.
Pat it and prick it
and mark it with 'B'.
And put it in the oven
for baby and me.

Old King Cole

Old King Cole
was a merry old soul,
And a merry old soul was he.
He called for his pipe,
And he called for his bowl,
And he called for
his fiddlers three.

This Little Piggy

This little piggy went to market,
This little piggy stayed at home.
This little piggy had roast beef,
This little piggy had none.
And this little piggy went,
"Wee, wee, wee, wee!"
All the way home.

Twinkle Twinkle Little Star

Twinkle, twinkle, little star,
How I wonder what you are.
Up above the world so high,
Like a diamond in the sky.
Twinkle, twinkle, little star,
How I wonder what you are.

That's enough singing for today.
It's time for bed.

Goodnight!